The Litter
BUG

Published under licence by Brown Dog Books and
The Self-Publishing Partnership Ltd, 10b Greenway Farm, Bath Rd,
Wick, nr. Bath BS30 5RL

www.selfpublishingpartnership.co.uk

ISBN printed book: 978-1-83952-470-7
ISBN e-book: 978-1-83952-471-4

Internal design by Andrew Prescott

Printed and bound in the UK

This book is printed on FSC certified paper

The Litter BUG

by Sam Barbour
illustrated by Kay Wong

BROWN
DOG
BOOKS

For my family

Foreword by Dr Cheri Chan

It is a joy to see a picture book written for Hong Kong children. Stories are a powerful way to enable children to learn language and develop thinking skills. Children love reading stories that have interesting characters, complex plots, playful use of language and beautiful artwork. All these elements make the reading experience and the learning process meaningful, engaging and fun. However, for many English language teachers in Hong Kong, it is not easy to source high quality authentic story books that are well written, beautifully illustrated with an exciting plot that'll keep the reader hooked from the beginning to the end. Until now! *The Litter Bug* by Sam Barbour is a magical story with strong interesting characters that the children will love and want to talk about. This book will provide teachers with numerous opportunities to generate rich conversations about Bud's adventures. As the children accompany Bud on his exciting and life-changing journey, they will have a chance to explore important themes such as friendship, family, community, identity, kindness, diversity, loss, acceptance, and so on. Children can be encouraged to share their personal responses to the themes through a wide variety of meaningful tasks. The beautiful illustrations by Hong Kong-based artist Kay Wong will also enrich children's aesthetic understanding of how images are used in picture books and help them make connections between visual and print texts.

Dr Cheri Chan
Hong Kong-based English Language Teacher Educator

CHAPTER 1
Stop Littering, Bud!

Friday 8th October. Kwai Fong Estate, New Territories, Hong Kong.

'Hurry up, Bud!' said Bud's mum. 'Or you'll be late, again.'

Dad strolled into the kitchen, kissed Mum's cheek and ruffled Bud's thick mop of jet-black hair. Bud seized his chance.

'Dad, can I have my pocket money early this week please?'

'Again?' said Mum, turning around sharply. 'It was the same last week.'

'After the breakfast you've just had you don't need to buy sweets, do you?' said Dad.

Dad waved his hands in the air and, as if by magic, pulled a crisp one-hundred dollar note from behind Bud's ear.

'Well, look at that!' said Dad, winking at Bud.

'Thanks,' said Bud. 'See you later!'

'Alligator!' said Dad.

'But no more littering,' pleaded Mum. 'I don't want more complaints from Mr Tong.'

Slam! The front door banged shut.

Bud set off slowly for school. The leaves and litter chased in circles in the quiet corners of the tall blocks of flats shooting up from the ground. As he turned a corner, people hurried past on their way to the MTR station but Bud dragged along in the opposite direction through the grove of banyan trees towards the main road.

Thump!

Bud kicked an empty cola can off the pavement, scuffing his new black shoes. Above, a huge advertising board read 'Keep Hong Kong Clean!' in bright letters.

Whoosh! Beep! Beep! Traffic zoomed past.

'Silly!' He smirked at a picture of a tiny yellow-and-black litter bug under the heading, *Don't be a Litter Bug!*

He sauntered into the nearby convenience store, spent most of his money and came out with armfuls of snacks. He stuffed them in his bag and arrived at the school gates two minutes late. The clock in the classroom seemed to be moving backwards but finally lunchtime arrived. Bud opened his school bag and gazed at his latest hoard of junk food glistening like pirate treasure. Two chocolate bars, one huge bag of sweets, a large packet of crisps and a lemon-flavoured Swiss roll all for him. He snatched the crisps and a chocolate bar and trotted into the playground to enjoy the recess. The happiest part of Bud's day had arrived. The playground buzzed and children ran here and there playing tag and basketball. Others skipped or played hopscotch. Bud shoved his way through the crowd before flopping onto a bench.

'Bye-bye, chocolate bar,' he said, tossing the empty wrapper onto the floor.

'Hey, Bud!' shouted James, his best friend. 'You can't do that.'

'Why?' asked Bud, scoffing bits of toffee and chocolate, which fell onto his shirt.

'Because it's wrong to litter,' boomed a deep voice from behind them.

Bud peered around to meet the friendly gaze of Mr Tong, the General Studies teacher. He smiled like a kind but all-knowing grandfather. Bud stood up, wiped the sweat off his face and twisted his fingers red with defiance.

'Sorry, Mr Tong,' said Bud.

'Never mind. Please pick it up and throw it in the rubbish bin.' said Mr Tong.

Bud picked up the wrapper and walked over to the bright blue rubbish bin next to the vending machines and threw it inside.

'Thank you, Bud,' said Mr Tong.

Bud smirked as Mr Tong walked away.

Honestly, why did everyone have to make so much fuss about a bit of plastic?

'I told you not to do it,' said James. 'But you *never* listen. You're a litter bug.'

'It's just a stupid wrapper,' said Bud. 'Who cares? Still friends?'

Bud gave James the large packet of crisps he'd bought earlier.

'Thanks, Bud,' said James. 'Yes, still friends, but you're too stubborn sometimes.'

James shared the crisps with Bud before throwing the empty packet into the rubbish bin. He played hopscotch for a while with his classmates but Bud just slouched back down again, fanning himself to cool off. The bell rang for the end of recess and James hurried back to his classroom with the rest of their classmates up the five flights of stairs. When they reached the fifth floor, Bud watched as his friends scampered to their classroom. He clung onto the green railing dragging himself along.

'I'm tired,' moaned Bud, struggling to keep up.

Sweat rolled off his forehead and he wiped his nose on his untucked shirt. During the General Studies lesson, Bud's class were learning about recycling and environmental protection.

'I'm bored,' announced Bud. 'Who cares about litter anyway?'

He sat in the corner of the classroom and stared out of the window, dreaming of catching and eating the fluffy candy floss clouds with little pink chocolate sprinkles on them that floated high above the classroom.

'We do! Dropping litter's bad and makes everywhere dirty,' answered Jenny, the Class Monitor.

'A poster will help to share the message, Bud,' said James.

'Waste of time!' Bud said, looking into his school bag to check on his stash.

Bud wasn't going to make a stupid poster. Instead, he carried on eating the candy floss clouds. He'd started work on the sun now as well, which was a huge yellow lollipop.

'Bud, come on! Don't be so stubborn,' urged Jenny.

Munch! Bud finished off his mid-afternoon imaginary snack.

'Just leave him, he's always like this,' said James. 'Come on, Jenny. Let's put up the posters on the notice board downstairs.'

'Bye, daydreamer,' said Jenny.

BRIINNNG! BRIINNNG!

The bell rang across the school corridors and, like a lightning flash, lit up thirty-six classrooms full of students itching for home time. The bell was followed by the thunderclap of students cascading out of school like a swollen river that had suddenly burst its banks. At last, the weekend had arrived. Bud trooped out of his classroom towards the next one, where Mr Tong was marking. Keep walking, head down, Bud chanted to himself as he sneaked past like a hungry mouse creeping past a sleeping cat.

'Be a good boy, Bud, and don't drop litter from now on, okay?' reminded Mr Tong, not even looking up from his desk.

Bud's stomach corkscrewed and plummeted like a supersonic roller-coaster. How did Mr Tong even know he was there? He slipstreamed out of the school gates, onto the street. Free at last from a long week of lessons, Bud gulped down the cool air as he jigged towards home. The area outside the school was still busy with a few straggling students followed by their nagging parents. The old people, who huddled around every day in all weathers playing Chinese chess and cards, shouted to each other enthusiastically. Bud chomped happily on his other chocolate bar and had stopped to watch the games when something twitched awkwardly in the corner of his eye.

'Oh, not her again,' said Bud, throwing the wrapper on the floor and starting to hurry away.

An ancient rag-picker woman stood a short distance in front of Bud. She sullenly scooped out plastic bottles and cans from a rubbish bin with her dirty, wrinkled hands and placed them in a torn, white-and-red bag. As Bud passed, she looked up and smiled but he just gave her an impolite stare, shaking his head as he hurried on.

'Weird old woman,' muttered Bud.

The old woman looked down and continued with her work. The wind picked up and bit at Bud's heels.

'Brrr,' complained Bud, pulling his jacket closely around his neck.

The next afternoon, Bud rushed out to spend the rest of his pocket money in the shops near his home. He started to eat the last few sweets from the huge bag he'd bought yesterday and as he did so, walked past the advertisement board again. 'Keep Hong Kong Clean!' He chewed as he wove a path in and out of the old streets and stalls just across the road from his school.

'Delicious!'

He finished the last sweet, throwing the empty sweet wrapper and bag onto the floor, ignoring the signs of 'No Littering' and the numerous bright orange litter bins. What could he buy today?

Maybe some jam doughnuts. As Bud turned the corner, he almost banged into the ancient rag-picker woman.

'Ah! You again. Watch out,' shouted Bud, jumping out of her way.

Smelly old rubbish woman, he thought. The old woman looked down and continued fishing out anything she could recycle from the grubby rubbish bin with her long walking stick. Her tatty bag was half full with plastic bottles.

'Sorry, Bud,' she said.

'Huh!' said Bud marching past.

Bud glanced back. That old woman was weird. She knew my name and she didn't even get out of my way.

CHAPTER 2

Strangely Sweet

Like a crocodile devouring its prey, Bud opened his mouth. The poor Swiss roll didn't stand a chance. It was gone in a single bite. He threw the plastic wrapper on the floor, watching it blow away in the wind that had started to pick up. A group of elderly ladies shook their heads, pointing at him with their long, aged fingers. Bud blundered on as the ancient rag-picker woman joined the huddle in their raucous complaints. Before he turned the corner, Bud glanced back and saw the group still jabbering away. Sometimes he wished he was invisible. Then maybe that strange old woman wouldn't get in his way and follow him. The next street was busy with people haggling and buying food from the nearby market.

Bud pushed on through the crowd, noticing damaged fruit and vegetables that had been accidently dropped onto the floor. Bud stepped carefully over a squashed tomato. Disgusting! The wind continued to blow litter around the street and the sun crept behind a dark cloud. Bud continued past the various little shops selling anything and everything. He shivered. It felt much colder here than near his home.

Beep! Beep! Bud's phone vibrated from inside his little bag.

He took out the shiny blue new phone that his parents bought him for his tenth birthday. There was a message.

'Don't be too long, Bud. You still have revision to do. Mum x'

It was nearly four o'clock on Saturday afternoon. He still had revision to do before his English and Chinese tests on Monday. Blah, blah, blah! They worried too much! Bud wasn't going home until he'd spent all his pocket money on snacks and guzzled them all down with soda. He put his phone back into his bag but forgot to zip it back up. There were fewer people about now. Something darted out from behind a rubbish bin in front of Bud.

'Cockroach!' Bud screamed.

Bud watched the cockroach scurry across the road and then something else caught his attention. On the corner of the street, there was a sweet shop! Bud crossed the street and laughed as he read its name out loud.

'Strangely Sweet!'

Sweets were meant to be sweet, but not *strange*. There was nothing strange about it at all. Except that he'd never seen the shop before. It seemed to have just sprung up out of nowhere. From the outside, it looked new but the swirly, colourful shop sign, window and door frames gave Bud a headache. He peered in the window, wondering if they sold doughnuts. The wind blew leaves in every direction. Still wary of the cockroach further down the street, he rushed through the door and into the shop. A bell above the door rang twice as he entered. Weirdly, it felt colder inside than outside and there was a strange musty smell of old cardboard. The light was quite dim but Bud could make out the tall and sinister figure of a grandfather clock in the corner. It chimed out four times in deep, deathly tones to signal four o'clock. Bud scanned the old, glass cabinets on his left-hand side. There were no doughnuts anywhere. He sighed and his stomach started to get that sinking feeling again. There was a flap of wings from the rafters high above and Bud felt he was being watched. The siren of a police car wailed in the distance, as if crying for help. Bud felt like he'd stepped into a time warp. What was this unusual shop? Maybe 'Strangely Sweet' was a good name for it after all. Bud scanned the shelves behind the counter and around the shop but everywhere was bare. The light flickered and a gigantic spider dangled from the counter in front of him.

'Ahhh!'

The spider continued spinning its web and Bud turned and headed for the door, his white sports shoes now covered in dust from the floor. He heard a voice.

'Ah! Bud. The greedy, lazy boy who likes to drop litter.'

How did she know him? How did she know his name? Bud jumped around and looked up, eyes darting from side to side. He dug deep red craters in his hands with his nails as he searched for the stranger's voice. On a high stool, behind the shop counter, an old woman was sitting gracefully reading a book. Her silvery hair fell down to her shoulders. Her voice was soft yet loud at the same time. Bud noticed her manner was kindly, like that of his late-grandmother who had passed away during the summer holidays. He thought briefly of Granny's smile as the woman's emerald green eyes shone brightly at Bud like shooting stars. A few, silent seconds passed as Bud twisted his fingers around. Then, the woman put down her book and stared. This was weird, creepy, and the woman made him shudder but he wouldn't show how scared he was. He folded his arms tight across his chest, took a deep breath and looked up.

'Me? Drop litter?' He laughed thinly. 'No! I never, ever drop litter! I'm always a good boy!'

'You're lying, Bud,' said the old woman.

'No, I'm not,' said Bud.

He tried to turn but his feet wouldn't move. Sweat started to roll off Bud's head. Why was it suddenly so hot? The old woman chuckled, picked up her book again and took a sip of tea from her beautifully ornate cup. The light flickered and the long-legged, black-and-yellow spider crept back into its dark crevice as if sensing that something was about to unfold.

'You're a litter bug, Bud,' said the old woman.

'No, I'm NOT!' repeated Bud.

He looked up as the wings of a brown owl ghosted from one wooden beam to another. Its large eyes stared silently at Bud. He tried to shuffle back but again his feet were set like concrete.

'Anyway, how do you know my name? Who are you?'

'I am just an old woman, and I've seen you throwing litter, outside your school and in other places,' she said, returning to her book.

'Really? So what?'

Who was this woman? Bud felt his heart freeze and drop into his stomach, his brain a whirlwind of confusion. He felt like a huge spotlight had been pointed on his face and he took out a tissue to mop his soaking brow. Bud's legs felt heavy and he tried to shake the tiredness out of them before leaving. The old woman took her walking stick from the counter and tapped it once on the floor. Bud was reaching for the door handle when he was immediately hypnotised by a bright flash. In an instant, a galaxy of sweets had appeared everywhere filling the shop with life and colour. Bud spotted tall, glass spaceship-looking jars high on the shelves.

'Wow!' he exclaimed as his annoyance and tiredness faded. 'What are they?

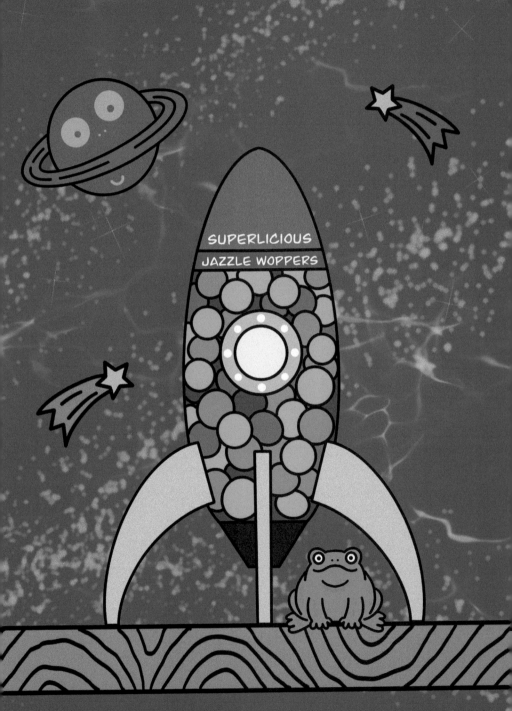

Chapter Three
The Magic Sweets

The owl continued to observe Bud from its high perch with its laser beam eyes and the wind whinnied furiously outside. Bud gazed at the sweets. The old woman's voice became distant, like the far moons of Jupiter. He was daydreaming again. This time, swimming in a rainbow river of sweets stocked with all the colours of the spectrum. The honeyed perfume of delicious candies drifted in the stale air and Bud floated along on his candy floss cloud. He popped a little pink chocolate sprinkle into his mouth and closed his eyes. All was well with the world. This was confectionery heaven and he certainly didn't want to come back down. A crack of thunder pierced Bud's garden of sweet, sugary serenity. The old woman chuckled again and shuffled over to him with the help of her beautiful walking stick, decorated with a curved handle in the shape of a horse's head, made from a deep orange wood.

'Ah yes! They're my most popular selection of sweets,' she said. 'What would you like?'

Her eyes radiated warmth now just like the walking stick. Strangely, the horse's face also seemed to match the old woman's. Bud, still coming down to Earth from Planet Sugar, couldn't reply immediately.

'Hmm, I don't know,' he stuttered. 'It's so difficult to choose.'

His bubble burst and he tumbled back into the real-world of endless questions and decisions.

He didn't want to choose. He wanted them all! That would be easier.

'There are SO many to choose from,' said Bud.

The old woman smiled again then took out a short, aluminium step-ladder and carefully climbed onto it.

'Wait a moment,' she said to Bud, ushering him to stand back a little.

The old lady's long, slender arms reached up and plucked a bright blue sweet from one of the spaceship jars on the top shelf. As she climbed down, she composed herself and offered it to Bud. A toad crawled out from behind the jar looking for a new hiding place.

'Here, try these,' she said. 'They're magic and taste wonderful.'

'Oooh! What are they?' squealed Bud.

The old woman chuckled again. The spider reappeared from its lair.

'They're called, Superlicious Jazzle Woppers!'

'Wow! I bet they taste good!' he said. 'I'll have twenty, please.'

'Perhaps it's wise for you to just buy one or two first,' said the old woman. 'Eating more can be dangerous.'

'What's dangerous about eating sweets?' he said.

'You have been warned, Bud.'

'Twenty Superlicious Jazzle Woppers, please!'

'Twenty dollars, please,' said the old woman. 'Thank you.'

Bud paid for the sweets with the last of his pocket money and immediately grabbed the packet. He was just about to rush out when the dim light-bulb flickered and the owl screeched. The woman looked up again sharply and, this time, the wind whistled angrily outside. The horse's head shifted to a darker colour. Bud's stomach twisted again.

'Remember, Bud, these sweets are magic...' she said. 'Everything will be fine as long as...'

The old woman's warning was interrupted by a deep rumble of thunder far-off in the distance. The horse's head turned black and a single bead of sweat dripped off Bud's head.

'As long as you throw your litter in the rubbish bin,' she continued quietly. 'Remember to call your parents and go home quickly.'

How did she know so much about him? Bud asked himself. He'd forgotten about buying doughnuts now. All he could REALLY think about was eating his new sweets.

'Okay!' he said, darting out of the shop, ignoring the red man traffic sign as he rushed across the road to the park.

Bud hurried on, sat on the nearest bench, tore off the blue sweet wrapper and stuffed the first sweet into his mouth. He was back on the way to Planet Sugar.

'Wow! What a taste! Wonderful! Yummy!' he exclaimed. 'They really ARE SUPERLICIOUS!'

There were not enough words for Bud to describe the taste of the Superlicious Jazzle Woppers. They were sweet yet a little sour, creamy but also bitter. The most exciting part was when you first popped it into your mouth and it tingled and fizzled on your tongue like a mini-firecracker before popping like a water balloon. It then sprayed a sugary fountain all around your mouth. In a few minutes, Bud had finished them all. In triumph, he then let out a huge burp that lasted for several seconds. He looked down at the empty sweet wrappers blowing away. The thunder began to draw nearer and he threw the last one onto the floor.

Chapter Four
Help!

Like an angry ghost, the wind shrieked around Bud's legs and the sky turned black. A huge explosion rang out across the entire park. Bud instinctively crouched into a ball. Before he knew it, lightning flashed across the heavens and thunder cracked overhead. The rain started to pour.

'Woah! What's going on?' he shouted, as a tornado of white smoke appeared, picked him up and spun him round like candy floss at a fairground.

'I feel dizzy!' he groaned.

Bud was now high in the air, pin-balling in all directions. Through the chaos and confusion, he heard the neighing of wild, angry horses. The tornado picked up speed, sucking up everything in its path, including branches, newspapers, cardboard boxes and the sweet wrappers that Bud had thrown away.

'Let me out of here,' he begged.

'Splat!' A Superlicious Jazzle Wopper sweet wrapper hit Bud as it whooshed into his mouth.

'Argh!' spluttered Bud, spitting it out.

He was hurled around in an endless cycle of loop-the-loops, as if he was in a huge washing machine.

'Oh no, not again,' groaned Bud.

The tornado eventually eased and Bud was churned out onto

the grass near the bench. The whinnying of the wild horses disappeared but the wind and the rain continued to howl. Bud lay motionless on the grass.

'I feel sick,' Bud cried.

Nobody could hear him. He managed to crawl out from underneath the last wisps of white smoke coughing and spluttering. What just happened? His head was still spinning and his face burnt red. Bud sat on the grass and looked around slowly. Why was everything so big? The park bench now towered above him and the rubbish bin seemed as tall as a skyscraper. Even the litter on the floor seemed bigger than Bud. He reached down to dust himself off and four limbs all moved at the same time.

'Argh!' he screamed. 'Get off me.'

Bud jumped back as if trying to fend off a huge giant squid but the more he squirmed, the more his new little arms and legs squiggled and wriggled. They were everywhere and it seemed like Bud had no control over their snake-like movements. After a struggle, he fell to the floor.

'What's happened to me? Someone, help.'

It must be a nightmare and surely he would wake up soon. He didn't though and nobody answered his call.

'Two legs and one, two, three, four arms!' said Bud as he slowly got used to moving his new limbs.

Both of his tiny feet had a tiny, dusty, white sports shoe but apart from that, they all looked the same. As he leaned forward to inspect them further, two stalks peered out at the front of his head, hitting him on the stomach.

'What's that?' He jolted back. 'Oh, more arms! On my face? Wait a minute, they look like antennae!'

Bud tried to stand and started pulling the arms, legs and antennae off his body. The harder he pulled, the more it hurt.

'Ow! Ow! Ow!' he repeated as he hopped around in a circle.

'Ow! Ow! Ow!'

The rain continued to lash down, bouncing off the bench and into Bud's eyes. Dark clouds shifted silently above. He soon got tired and scuttled under the bench.

'Oh! I give up,' he said.

CLAAANG!

The sound of something heavy hitting the metal bench above Bud's head was deafening and he covered his ears. The vibrations lasted several seconds. What was that? Bud crouched and saw a pair of huge shoes shuffling about in front of him. He strained his neck looking upwards at the giant and two green eyes smiled at him warmly from above.

'Hello Bud!' said the voice.

Bud's heart froze. Even his hands and head dare not sweat. For a moment he couldn't move or utter a single sound. He edged towards the far end of the bench. The beautiful emerald eyes continued to observe Bud curiously as a cat watches a mouse. There was a familiar sparkle to them. He'd seen those eyes before, but where? He frantically tried to remember but, just then, a huge, dirty, wrinkled hand came wriggling under the bench towards him. It was three times the size of Bud's whole body. He clung to the outside of one of the back legs of the bench, trying not to get washed away by the downpour.

'Come out, Bud. I just want to talk to you,' said the voice.

Bud was terrified that the giant knew his name. There was no way he was going to go out. The giant's hand scuttled from side to side like a hungry crab before retreating. Bud sighed and wiped his face. His sharp eyes patrolled the front of the bench for any more sign of movement. His feet were soaked and he felt completely exhausted, utterly alone and miserable. Behind him, the rain and wind continued turning the sky into a raging black hole. It would be dangerous to make a run for it so he stayed put. He began to feel sleepy.

SCRAATCCHH!

A huge horse's head now came under the bench swaying slowly from side to side. Every time it moved, it made a sickening scraping and scratching sound and looked dark and angry. Sooner or later, it was going to hook Bud from under the bench and then what? He was trapped and had to do something.

Chapter Five
Bud the Litter Bug

CLAAANG!

The heavy head of the horse clattered against the bench leg Bud was holding

'Ahh!' he cried and sprinted out from the far side of the bench.

With six limbs he was surprisingly fast and, within minutes, he'd reached the long grass a few metres away. A shower of raindrops caught in the blades of grass exploded onto Bud like water balloons. He collapsed in a heap and caught his breath. He had used up all his remaining energy and was now completely drained. Phew, that was close. It mustn't have seen him escape. Bud peeked through the grass as the giant used its walking stick to fish out plastic bottles from the rubbish bin near the bench. The rain had eased but the cool autumn wind was still blowing his litter all across the park. Bud recognised the giant. It was the smelly old rubbish woman!

Crack! Another Superlicious Jazzle Wopper wrapper hit his face.

'Ow!' he howled.

Bud watched it blow away. He looked around. He was all alone. Chitter, chatter. The sound of Bud's tiny teeth rattled in the cold. He couldn't stop shaking. 'Help me! Anyone, please help me!'

His tiny voice was drowned out in the unforgiving wind. The park stretched in all directions.

'I don't want to die here,' he cried. 'I want to go home.'

He hauled himself up with the help of a broken twig and started walking. Bud hacked through the soaking wet grass as he tramped along miserably towards the path.

SPLISH! SPLOSH! SPLISH! SPLOSH!

The park entrance felt like it would take hours to reach. He reached the path, glanced back at the ancient rag-picker woman one more time and then saw a huge creature appear in the distance.

What was that?

Another giant had come out of nowhere! Bud squinted.

It was a man, striding towards him from the adjacent basketball court. He was surging towards the park entrance and, as he marched along, he crushed leaves and litter alike under his giant blue sports shoes. Bud shuddered. He needed to hide – and fast. Either that or get crushed! As in the sweet shop, something held his feet there as the giant approached. Bud knew he was in danger but was strangely hypnotised by the man's approach. As he got closer and closer, the man was talking nervously into his mobile phone as if he had lost something or someone. Bud tried to study his face in more detail but it was impossible. He was too tall and was getting dangerously close now. So much so that Bud could make out the brand of the shoes he was wearing. Bud scurried off the path and looked for a place to hide.

He found an empty plastic water bottle in the grass verge. He hid behind it watching and waiting for the giant to go past. Crunching along, in huge strides, the giant was only metres away now. He'd put his mobile phone away and was shouting in all directions.

'Where are you?'

He knew that voice! It sounded deafening to his tiny ears but there was no mistaking it. For some reason, Bud had no fear now but, instead, a strange sense of excitement filled his heart. He stood up and walked out from behind the plastic bottle.

'Where are you?' the man continued.

Bud's six limbs started to wriggle furiously. It was Mr Tong his General Studies teacher! Bud leapt up and down.

'Mr Tong! Mr Tong!' he shouted. 'It's me! Bud!'

Without even looking down, Mr Tong hurried past the plastic bottle towards a small clump of bushes further along the path.

'There you are,' said Mr Tong. 'Naughty dog, I've been looking everywhere for you.'

A beautiful brown puppy leapt out of the bushes towards Mr Tong. Its tail wagged from side to side. Mr Tong put the puppy back on the lead and walked out of the park towards the direction of the main road. He couldn't see Bud or hear his tiny voice.

'I'm here. Down here!' Bud tried one last time.

Bud fell to the floor, put his head in his hands and sobbed.

'I want to go home,' he cried clutching his stomach.

THUD! THUD! THUD! THUD!

Bud glanced back and saw the ancient rag-picker woman stand up and stutter along towards Bud. The walking stick pounded off the path, each time getting louder.

'Oh no!' he cried. 'She's coming to get me.'

Bud hurried towards the park entrance. The sky darkened and the cool wind felt colder around Bud's little neck, arms and legs. After what seemed like two hours, he crossed the road, feeling dizzy, his head aching. He'd lost his little blue rucksack and everything in it, including his new phone and beautiful cashmere scarf. It must have got lost during the explosion. The wind continued and the streets were chillingly silent. He looked up briefly and saw the yellow streetlamps bearing down on him. His shadow was tiny. The buildings and street signs seemed to gang up on him like older, playground bullies. It was past sunset and he felt really cold and small, like a tiny mouse in a great, dark forest. Noises from distant traffic blared in the distance and Bud thought he could hear a horse neighing. He glanced back. A crooked, shadowy figure was crossing the road. Bud pressed on. He still had a long way to go to reach home and he wasn't sure how to get there. Everywhere looked the same. Bud had arrived at the entrance of a dark and dirty alley, which stretched as far as he could see. In the haze, it was a gateway to a ghostly world. Was this the right way? Bud paused. He jumped up and down, hugging himself to keep warm.

Stomp! Stomp!

The sound of heavy footsteps came from around the corner.

Bud shuddered. Who was it?

STOMP! STOMP! STOMP! STOMP!

The footsteps got closer. After some hesitation, Bud scrambled forwards, making his way deep into the bowels of the filthy alley.

Chapter Six
The Dark and Dirty Alley

Bud didn't look back as the loud footsteps of a man marched past the opening of the alley. After the sound faded, the alley became still again except for the soft whirring of the air conditioners high on the walls of the old factory buildings on both sides.

Drip! Drip! Drop! Drip! Drip! Drop!

The sound of water falling from the air conditioners was like seconds ticking on a clock, reminding Bud that it was late and he was in deep trouble. Everything seemed huge, dirty and smelly as he trudged along avoiding the deep puddles and water gushing down the gutters on both sides. Head down, keep walking, he kept reminding himself. His tiny feet pitter-pattered on the wet floor. The alley was narrower now and there were huge bags of overflowing rubbish everywhere so Bud had to work harder to avoid stepping on anything dirty. He'd wandered into a nightmare, a Halloween-like maze with no easy way out. He was so tired, his tiny head throbbed and the stench made him dizzy and irritable. Why was it so smelly?

'It stinks,' said Bud as he held his nose.

The last word reverberated around the alley. Then, out of the darkness sprang a huge brown cockroach!

'Who are YOU? You woke me up!' shouted the cockroach.

'You can speak?' said Bud, almost falling backwards.

'Of course I can speak,' growled the cockroach. 'What do you want?'

The realisation struck Bud that his nightmare just turned a lot worse. His heart was racing.

'Stay away from me you horrible, dirty cockroach!'

The grumpy cockroach's face turned black. In one magnificent leap, it landed in front of Bud, blocking his way. It stood firm, folded its long, thin arms and let out a loud sigh.

'How dare you talk to ME like that! My name is DARING Mr Cockroach, not a dirty one!'

'S...S...Sorry, Daring Mr Cockroach, it's just that I'm so scared,' stuttered Bud, shivering.

Daring Mr Cockroach scratched its big head for a moment before nodding in bemused acknowledgement.

'Scared...of a cockroach? Whatever next? Never mind,' he said. 'Wait here...'

Daring Mr Cockroach then turned his back dramatically and leaped towards a large pile of black bin bags overflowing with days-old rubbish.

'Old Mr Rat, come and see our new neighbour.'

Nothing stirred except the constant drone of the air conditioners above.

'Old Mr Rat! Old Mr Rat!' shouted Daring Mr Cockroach.

A wise-looking, bespectacled rat hobbled out, with a lollipop stick as a walking stick, into the light of the now full autumn moon.

'What's the matter, Daring Mr Cockroach? I'd just nodded off you know,' he said, rubbing his eyes.

'Oh, goodness, hello, what's your name?' Old Mr Rat asked, suddenly noticing Bud shivering in the middle of the alley.

Bud turned away. Surely, it must be a terrible nightmare. Animals couldn't talk! Bud rubbed his face and pinched himself hard on one of his four arms.

'Ow!'

He wasn't dreaming. Bud turned to speak to the rat and wrung his four hands red raw.

'My name's B... B... Bud.'

A police car whooshed past the alley with its sirens wailing, the sounds ricocheting like pinging bullets hurting Bud's sensitive ears. By now, a large mosquito and a thin worm had joined the gathering from behind a soggy cardboard box. They started to fly and wriggle towards Bud.

'Hi! I'm Mickey Mosquito,' buzzed Mickey. 'We heard Daring Mr Cockroach shouting.'

'I'm Miss Worm, welcome to our home!'

Bud stepped back instinctively. From behind a broken TV,

leapt an empty can of cola.

'Hi B... B... Bud! My name's Crazy Cola!' he said, as he pirouetted up and down on the TV.

What's happening? Maybe Bud banged his head at the park and was imagining everything.

Crazy Cola continued to leap, twist and turn before letting out a huge burp and falling flat on his back.

'That's why he's called CRAZY Cola,' said Old Mr Rat shaking his head and smiling.

The living nightmare was getting worse and it was a long way until morning. A bruised green apple appeared from under a broken shopping trolley. It stumbled over to them wearily with its head down.

'Hello, Bud,' it said. 'I'm Fruity.'

Bud felt the floor move and the alley spin. Not again! He was trapped in a never-ending circus freak show. He swayed from side to side and the tall buildings danced above his dizzy head. His eyes were so heavy.

'Woah!' he wailed.

All sounds merged into one huge, faraway monotone. He looked around to see the strange alley gang surrounding him and peering curiously at their new visitor. In the distance, the same crooked shadowy figure hobbled towards them.

THUD! DRIP! THUD! DROP! THUD! WHIR! THUD! THUD!

BANG!

This was the end. Bud fainted and hit the ground.

Chapter Seven
New, Unexpected Friends

After a few seconds, Bud came to and looked around wearily.

'Oh! The poor thing's terrified! Are you okay?' asked Miss Worm.

Slowly, as Bud gathered his senses, he saw all these strange creatures, staring with beady eyes. Bud leapt up and moved backwards. His body began to shake and he covered his face, hoping they would all go away.

'Ahh! Don't hurt me. Please! Let me go!' he cried, as he tried to get off the tin.

'We won't hurt you. Are you our new neighbour?' asked Mickey Mosquito.

Bud stopped shaking and peered out.

'No! I mean, I don't think so. Where am I?'

Old Mr Rat stepped forward slowly and smiled.

'This is our home, the dark and dirty alley.'

Miss Worm leaned forward and studied Bud.

'Wow! Look at your markings! You're a litter bug, aren't you?' she said. 'I've heard of litter bugs, I've seen them in pictures but you're the first one I've actually met!'

'A litter bug?' exclaimed Bud checking himself again and then gaping around.

'Yes, that's right. I've only seen them on advertisement boards,' said Old Mr Rat.

Daring Mr Cockroach held up the lid of an empty soda bottle for Bud to look at his colourful reflection. On his back, Bud had a beautiful yellow-and-black striped shell.

The old woman at Strangely Sweet was right. Bud really was a litter bug but how and why? Was this some sort of magic trick? Everyone tried to shake Bud's many hands and legs all at the same time.

'No, step back, don't touch me,' said Bud. 'I need to go home, now! Where's Kwai Fong Estate?'

Fruity looked up and pointed further down the alley. Bud stared.

'Down to the end of the alley, turn right and keep walking,' it said. 'It's very far away.'

'Thank you, Fruity. Bye, everyone,' said Bud.

He turned and started walking

BUMP!

He slipped on the green slime of the wet floor.

'Ow!'

Bud grunted and slammed all four hands on the floor as he tried to stand up but kept falling back down.

'This alley's so dirty and smelly,' he shouted. 'There's rubbish everywhere!'

Crazy Cola helped Bud up, looked at him funnily and laughed.

'How can you live here?' Bud shouted, pointing to some rubbish nearby and holding his nose.

'Well, that's very interesting! A litter bug that doesn't like litter!' said Mickey Mosquito.

'Sounds normal to me!' said Crazy Cola.

'Well, we LOVE litter…don't we everyone?' shouted Daring Mr Cockroach.

'Yes, we do!' chorused the friends.

Bud's face twisted as he watched the motley crew of alley creatures dance a little jig around him. The evening rain began to fall, making even bigger puddles in the dark and dirty alley. Bud's clothes were soaked and he was tired and hungry. How was he ever going to get out of here?

Chapter Eight
The Bin Lorry

Old Mr Rat looked at the sky and nodded solemnly at Miss Worm.

'It's late and cold. Winter will soon arrive.'

'Bud, please make yourself at home,' said Old Mr Rat as he stretched out his hands to a decaying heap of damp newspapers and cardboard boxes.

'Thank you,' said Bud. 'But I need to get back to my family.'

'Just don't wake me up, again!' Daring Mr Cockroach smiled at Bud, hitting him gently on the shoulder.

'I won't,' Bud replied.

It was hours since he finished off the sweets and he was ravenous. There was nothing to eat here, he decided, scanning the rubbish bags for food. Miss Worm wriggled over and smiled.

'If you're feeling peckish, there's a half-empty packet of crisps!' she said, looking down at the snack on the floor. 'Spicy cheese, my favourite.'

Bud scurried over, sat down and started eating the broken crisps that were still in the packet.

'They're so soggy,' he said, attacking his third crisp.

'Where do you sleep?' There's rubbish everywhere!'

Old Mr Rat smiled.

'We all sleep in the rubbish, Bud. As you're a litter bug, perhaps you should too.'

Crunch! Crunch! Munch! Munch!

Bud was hungry and continued eating the crisps but they tasted disgusting and he held back his urge to vomit.

'You should feel at home here,' Miss Worm said, softly.

She stood up and looked for a place for Bud to sleep. Bud had finished eating and shivered in the growing dark and cold. The buildings all seemed bigger and hard-edged at night. The alley was a scary, alien world and no place for a tiny litter bug. He should never have come here. Everything had changed after he ate the sweets in the park, but why? A hundred questions flooded his brain. His mind was in a mess and he held his face in his hands and wept.

'I want to be a boy again,' he cried as tears began to fall.

'HEY! He's crazy just like ME!' exclaimed Crazy Cola.

'Please, Crazy Cola, be polite,' urged Old Mr Rat.

'He thinks he's a boy,' Crazy Cola continued as he pirouetted and twisted around the rubbish bags once more.

'I want my mummy!' said Bud, stomping his feet in his own little lake of tears.

Bud stood and ran towards the entrance of the alley. Everyone paused and remained silent, with only the rain, the air-conditioners and Bud's little feet making any sound. As he got closer to the entrance, the whoosh of the passing taxis and the thud of the driving rain got louder. Bud ran on, nearly there now. The night dragged on, with the alley bathed in a dark yellow glow from the streetlamps confirming that morning was still very far away. He was almost free from the nightmare of the dark and dirty alley. He stopped and shuddered. What was that sound?

Bud froze. Just ahead, the ancient rag-picker woman was sleeping on a flattened cardboard box with her red-and-white bag of plastic bottles and tin cans acting as a pillow. Her horse's head walking stick lay at her side, its face facing towards him. Was she following him? Bud tip-toed past, watching closely for any tiny movement. He reached the entrance of the alley and glanced back one more time.

Whoosh! Whoosh!

Something rumbled in the distance. Bud jumped.

VROOM! WHOOSH!

The sound was louder now.

VROOM! WHOOSH! VROOM! WHOOSH!

A huge, yellow bin lorry turned into the alley. Bud couldn't move. He was blinded by the flash of the lorry's headlamps. Then he realised what had happened. Bud turned and sprinted back down the murky alley.

'Oh no,' he screamed. 'Help!'

NEIGH! NEIGH!

As he passed the ancient rag-picker woman, her horse-head walking stick let out an ear-piercing neigh. She immediately stirred, opened her eyes and sat up. Bud felt he was being watched closely. The walking stick was so familiar! Could it be the same as the old woman's from Strangely Sweet? Bud's mind was in such a flutter that he even imagined they were the same person! Impossible! The ancient rag-picker woman stood up and shuffled on behind.

SPLAT!

Another Superlicious Jazzle Wopper wrapper covered Bud's face for an instant. Everything went dark.

'Get off me!' Bud cried. 'What! Another one!'

VROOM! WHOOSH! VROOM! WHOOSH!

The lorry changed gear and roared like a giant robotic wave. It accelerated through the dark depths of the alley. The bin lorry was right behind him now. Its huge mechanical brushes were sweeping up rubbish on both sides of the alley. Bud could hear them but he daren't look back.

SPLASH!

'Ahh!' he shouted, as dirty water from the gutter sprayed all over him.

Bud had no time to clean himself off. He scoured the alley in front of him for any sign of his friends but the scene was deserted. Bud felt the rush of air behind him and the heat of the headlights bearing down like laser beams. He kept running, zig-zagging to the sides but there was rubbish everywhere. There was nowhere to hide and no one to help.

BANG!

Bud closed his eyes. The impact of the big red brush sent him whirling into the air.

'I'm going to die,' cried Bud, as he spun round. 'Mummy!'

SMACK!

A piece of rotten banana skin slapped Bud in the face.

'Oww!'

Bud peeled the banana skin off his face but more rubbish flew into Bud's eyes, ears and mouth from all directions. He was suffocating.

'Ahh, I can't breathe,' Bud cried.

He landed on a huge heap of waste inside the hungry belly of the bin lorry, gasping for breath. The great metal monster surged forwards, hoovering up everything in its path. A powerful jet spray from under its body then cleaned the walls and floor with clean water. The dark and dirty alley glistened. As the bin lorry continued to fill up, the weight of rubbish pressed down on Bud. He couldn't see, he couldn't breathe. He would die in here, buried alive. Images of home and his parents flickered in his mind before everything faded to black.

Chapter Nine
Going to the Port

PLOP! PLOP!

The sound of the last remaining raindrops hit the outside of the bin lorry.

'Oh, my head,' groaned Bud.

Bud sat up against an empty milk carton, rubbed his eyes and glanced at himself again. It wasn't a bad dream after all but a living nightmare. Bud's body ached all over and his hollow stomach reminded him of the danger he was now in. Miss Worm suddenly appeared from underneath a flattened banana box and wriggled over to him.

'Bud! Why are you here?' she exclaimed.

'Miss Worm!' said Bud. 'I... I... don't know, where are we?

Miss Worm started to root around in the rubbish bags.

'We got caught by a bin lorry,' she said, nudging a tiny piece of stale bread towards him with her nose. 'The others are still asleep over there, look.'

'Oh yes, I remember now,' said Bud as he munched the bread and glanced at the friends all snoring in a messy heap.

'Where are we going?'

SQUAWK! SQUAAAWK!

A seagull landed on the roof of the bin lorry, its feet making a horrible scratching sound. Bud started shaking and Miss Worm leaned over to protect him.

TAP! TAP! TAP! TAP!

The seagulls started to attack the roof with their strong beaks. Miss Worm smiled kindly.

'I'm not sure, Bud,' said Miss Worm. 'I've never been in a bin lorry before.'

'We have to escape,' cried Bud. 'I need to get home.'

The bin lorry stopped and Bud and Miss Worm were thrown into a mountain of empty plastic bottles.

'Ow!' cried Miss Worm as she helped Bud to sit up. 'We've arrived.'

The huge metal door of the bin lorry heaved open with a terrifying screech and the floor tilted upwards. Miss Worm leapt up.

'Hold on to me, Bud,' she said. 'Hey! Wake up, you lot.'

Rays of light streamed into the lorry as the door opened wider. Bud closed his eyes. He could smell the sea and the overpowering acrid smell of decaying rubbish. Seagulls screamed wildly above him. Their eyes looked cruel and hungry. He felt so small. Miss Worm clambered over the rubbish towards the rest of the group. Bud followed.

'Look, it's Bud!' cried Crazy Cola, jumping up.

'We thought you'd gone,' said Daring Mr Cockroach.

'Get ready,' said Old Mr Rat.

The creatures just had time to greet Bud before the door flung open and he saw huge containers, tall buildings and gigantic boats spread out everywhere like different-coloured tentacles of a huge jellyfish. The noises were deafening. Bud clutched Miss Worm's waist and Old Mr Rat's hand tightly.

CREEEAAAK!

The metal door groaned as it locked in place high above them.

'Here we go,' Miss Worm shouted. 'Heads down and stay together.'

In an avalanche of rubbish, they tumbled to the front of the lorry and then out into the open air.

'Ahh, help!' cried Bud, waving his arms and legs.

Somersaulting through mid-air, the group crash-landed onto a pile of decaying tyres with a soft bump. They were near the edge of a very deep container filled with waste of all sorts. Seagulls dive-bombed them in waves of two or three at a time, screeching like terrible harpies.

SQUAWK! SQUAAAWK!

The friends clambered underneath the tyres for safety but, before Bud could look up, he was plucked from the group in a long, bamboo fishing net.

'Miss Worm, help!' cried Bud. 'Where am I going?'

'No Bud! Come back,' said Miss Worm, clutching onto the net.

SQUAWK! SQUAAAWK!

A huge black-eyed seagull screamed, closing in on the net. It caught Miss Worm in its beak but she managed to wriggle free, landing back on the tyres and looking up helplessly.

'Bud!' she shouted. 'Watch out!'

'Go away,' shouted Bud, kicking madly at the net where the seagull was still attacking.

SQUAWK! SQUAAAWK! SQUAWK! SQUAAAWK!

The seagull circled back for another assault as more gathered above. The din was unrelenting and Bud's head pounded. As the net rose quickly, Bud watched his friends burying deeper into the mountain of stinking rubbish to escape the marauding birds.

'Goodbye, my friends,' he cried, wiping a tear away.

Bud fainted and fell motionless into the bottom of the net.

Chapter Ten
Setting Sail

BOOOOOOOOM! BOOOOOOOOM! BOOOOOOOOM!

'What was that?' cried Bud, leaping up and falling down again.

The three long blasts of its loud horn announced the barge's departure. The boat heaved forwards and Bud held on to the net for safety. He glanced up and saw the ancient rag-picker woman sitting on a small metal seat next to him. What was she doing here? She took out a comb from her bag to brush her long silver hair. Bud watched as her emerald eyes glistened in the reflection off the waves and her horse-head walking stick hung on the railing. It seemed to be watching him. Was it the old woman from Strangely Sweet or the ancient rag-picker woman or both? It was so confusing but why did she catch him in the net? She peered down at Bud.

NEIGH! NEIGH!

The walking stick made that horrible neighing sound again and turned jet black.

'Calm down, Skye,' said the rag-picker. 'Don't be so stubborn.'

'Hello, Bud,' she said. 'It's me, the smelly old rubbish woman.'

Bud loosened his grip on the netting and looked up.

'I'm sorry I called you that,' cried Bud as he struggled to stand in the soft net. 'Please don't hurt me.'

'I won't,' she said. 'I promise.'

'Where am I? Where are my friends?' said Bud, looking around.

'We're on a refuse barge and your friends are in there somewhere,' said the rag-picker. 'Snoring their heads off.'

In front of them lay rows and rows of neatly stacked containers stretching to the front of the boat. On the port side, there was a small collection of loose refuse, ropes and other things. The bobbing sensation of being on the water turned Bud's face light green.

'Where? I can't see them.'

'Near the ropes, there,' said the old woman, pointing. 'They dug down so far I couldn't see them at first,'

'To escape the seagulls, I remember,' said Bud. 'Let's go and fetch them.'

'Let them sleep first, I'll pick them up when we get off.'

'Can you not just collect them now?' said Bud, frantically look around him. 'The seagulls could come back at any minute.'

'Don't worry,' she said. 'They'll be fine.'

'Where are we going?' said Bud.

'You'll see,' said the rag-picker. 'Let's get you out of that net.'

The ancient rag-picker woman chuckled and gently offered a hand for Bud to sit on. Slowly, Bud climbed into the palm of the wrinkled hand and was placed carefully on the seat next to her. Bud studied the woman's face. She looked like the ancient rag-picker woman but also the woman from Strangely Sweet. Why was that? She couldn't be both, could she? He started to sweat again and wrung his tiny hands. He had a weird feeling. She smiled, her eyes twinkling brightly once more and Bud started to settle into his new environment. He brushed himself off, cleaned his face and sat, cross-legged, staring at the walking stick.

CLANG! CLANG!

The walking stick jolted furiously on the railing. The old woman clicked her fingers and a ray of sunshine shone gently in Skye's face and calmed him. She turned to Bud.

'First things first! Introductions. Call me Helen,' she said, holding out her hand. 'This is Skye, my faithful friend. It's okay, you can pat him, he won't bite!'

'Nice to meet you, both,' said Bud, warily patting Skye on the head.

Skye neighed with approval and smiled, his head glowing with rich amber tones.

'What just happened?' said Bud.

'You all got caught up in a bin lorry and taken to a Transfer Station in the city,' said Helen.

'What's a Transfer Station?' asked Bud, looking back towards the quayside.

'It's where all the rubbish people throw away is processed,' said Helen. 'Now, didn't I tell you those sweets were magic?' she continued.

'What?' said Bud, almost falling off Helen's hand.

'I also told you not to drop litter,' continued Helen.

'I didn't drop litter,' said Bud.

'Now, now,' said Helen. 'We both know that's a lie.'

Bud shrugged and turned away, looking down at the waves. He was always terrible at telling lies and he knew it. Helen chuckled and plucked Skye from the railings.

'I don't know what you're talking about,' said Bud.

'You're lying, Bud,' said Helen. 'Again!'

The wrinkles disappeared from her face and she seemed more energetic than before. The barge was in the open water now and the skyscrapers got smaller. The wind blew in her long, silver hair. She strolled down the deck leaving Bud alone. A sailor dressed in smart white uniform strode towards them. Skye started to whinny softly.

'Good morning, Helen,' he said, walking past.

'Good morning, John.'

'A cockroach,' he shouted as he saw Bud on the seat.

He took out a small, fluorescent green bottle from his jacket pocket and sprinted towards where Bud was sitting. Bud turned round just in time to notice a giant aiming a monstrous bottle at him. The words, *Super Pesticide Spray* and *TOXIC* were splashed in big black letters on the front, under a picture of a dead cockroach. The sailor took aim. Bud looked down. Helen tapped her walking stick once on the deck.

'Ahh!' shouted Bud, leaping off the seat.

The barge splashed into the bigger waves. John stepped back. Bud had disappeared.

'Oh, it's gone,' said John. 'It must have flown away.'

'Never mind, thanks anyway, John.' said Helen, walking back. 'How long until we arrive?'

'It could be two hours as the waterways are busy today,' said John.

The sailor continued on his inspection towards the centre of the barge and disappeared down the stairs. Helen slowly sat down again and looked underneath the seat. Clinging tightly to the underside of the seat like a ninja spider, was Bud.

'Well done,' said Helen, as he clambered out and back on to the seat again.

'Why didn't you help me?' gasped Bud, still struggling for breath. 'I was nearly killed.'

'Why did you lie to me, Bud?' said Helen. 'It's not the first time.'

Helen raised her eyebrows and winked at Skye before staring firmly at Bud for a few seconds in silence. For once, Bud had nothing to say. He stared defiantly at Helen before she smiled and looked away.

'You got yourself into this mess, and now you need to get yourself out of it.'

Chapter Eleven
The Open Sea

It was mid-morning and heavy traffic congested the busy sea lanes around Victoria Harbour. The barge detoured slowly under the Tsing Ma Bridge and then past Chep Lap Kok Airport before sailing down the west coast of Lantau Island. They'd just passed under the huge Hong Kong-Zhuhai-Macau Bridge. The swell of the waves swayed the barge from side to side, spraying white water on to the deck every few seconds. Bud was clinging to the railings at the back of the barge.

'My stomach,' cried Bud. 'I'm going to be sick.'

Bud looked over towards the bow end of the barge where Helen was doing a little jig and tapping Skye on the ground. He felt even worse.

'I need to get off this thing,' he spluttered, before I fall in and drown.'

Helen returned holding two enormous strawberry jam doughnuts. Bud saw them and held his stomach again. Where did she get those? Who on earth would want to eat doughnuts here?

'Want one?' asked Helen. 'Extra jam in these. Delicious.'

Skye snorted with approval. The sound of the wind, waves and Bud's rolling stomach swished and sploshed in his tiny ears. Bud's head was a mess and he could feel the inexorable creep of vomit up his throat. It seemed that Helen the ancient rag-picker was probably also the owner of Strangely Sweet but how? All he knew was that she knew a lot about him and it might be better to be honest with her from now on, whoever she was. His head throbbed with pain and another hundred questions.

'No, thanks,' said Bud.

'Okay!' said Helen. 'I'll have to finish them both then.'

'I remember what happened the last time you gave me something to eat,' said Bud.

'I did warn you not to eat too many, didn't I?' said Helen.

Bud couldn't reply. He groaned and staggered to the railings like a boxer after twelve rounds. He looked over his shoulder at his beautiful yellow-and-black shell which had also changed green and white with seasickness. He started to lose the sensation in his legs.

'First time on a boat?' asked Helen, finishing off the second doughnut.

'Yes,' groaned Bud.

Bud couldn't stand it anymore and vomited over the side of the boat, wiped his mouth then slumped to the floor with one hand still holding on to the railing. The vomit, like the Superlicious Jazzle Woppers was bright blue and the vile taste of soggy crisps and stale bread was overpowering. Helen looked at Bud and shook her head.

'I told you to buy one first, not twenty. Remember?'

Helen picked up Bud and together they looked over the railings at the rippling chop of white water churning and frothing behind the boat. He stared at the wake and clung to Helen's ancient thumb.

'You're not going to throw me in are you?' asked Bud. 'How can I change back into a boy and go home?

'Like I said, you need to help yourself,' said Helen. 'Look!'

Bud sat down and crossed his feet in frustration. He wasn't getting anywhere.

'Can you see the dead fish?' she said, pointing to the dozens of upturned white bellies floating around the debris.

'Yes,' said Bud. 'Why did they die?'

'Pollution,' said Helen.

Bud scratched his head and vaguely remembered the word from his General Studies lessons.

'What's that?' he asked.

'It's when people don't dispose of their rubbish properly,' said Helen.

'Like throwing it into the sea?' asked Bud.

'Yes, or on the floor,' said Helen, piercing Bud with her sharp eyes.

Bud felt the ice-cold force of Helen's words. A pang of discomfort made his stomach shudder for a moment. He stared closely at the water.

'Look!' cried Bud.

Floating past the barge, was a dead seagull. A plastic ring hung round its neck. Poor bird. Bud looked down and played with his fingers as he briefly thought of his own littering. Holding Bud safely in her hand, Helen walked up the side of the long barge. There was so much waste. Bud scanned the small heap for any sign of his friends.

'Where will this rubbish go?' asked Bud.

'Some of it will be burned in a giant incinerator and some buried in landfill,' said Helen.

Bud started to sweat and tiny beads fell onto Helen's furrowed hands.

'Why are you taking me here? What about my friends?' he cried, tears starting to flow.

'I want to teach you more about rubbish,' said Helen. 'Don't worry, I'm taking you all back on the return barge.'

'Phew,' sighed Bud. 'I want to be a boy again. Can you help me?'

'That depends,' said Helen.

BOOOOOOOOM!

The barge's horn blasted out to warn passing ships and Bud covered his tiny ears.

'On what?' he shouted.

'On whether you can learn the lessons of your previous mistakes,' said Helen.

'All this rubbish, all this mess wasn't just down to me!' said Bud. 'I only dropped a few sweet wrappers. It wasn't my fault.'

'Every action has a consequence,' said Helen. 'Even small actions.'

Bud crossed his arms and looked away. This was crazy. Just a terrible dream. Sooner or later he would wake up, wouldn't he? But as Bud stared into the vortex of white water crashing furiously below, he knew it was all too real.

Chapter Twelve
A Lucky Escape

The barge continued to chug along towards the tiny coastal village of Tai O. A pair of white-bellied sea-eagles soared effortlessly above them, looking for food. The sea breeze was invigorating and Bud started to perk up after being sick earlier.

'Over there!' cried Bud, pointing towards the rocky shore.

Two pink dolphins leapt out of the water and splashed back down. They seemed to be playing a game of *catch*. As they jumped they span around, the sun shone on their backs and, in an instant, they'd dived back under the water.

'Pink dolphins,' said Helen. 'They're so beautiful but now, sadly endangered.'

'Because of pollution?' asked Bud.

'Yes,' said Helen. 'When I was a young girl, there were so many of them.'

Bud clambered back up to the top of Helen's thumb to try and get another glimpse. Where were they? The dolphins jumped up again, this time much closer to the barge. A short distance away, a large, ugly knot of plastic rubbish was bobbing up and down on the waves towards them. A small white egret struggled to stand on the floating plastic island as it pecked for food.

'They're going to swim into the rubbish,' cried Bud. 'We need to warn them!'

One of the dolphins jumped out again and landed on the plastic flotsam. His long, thin body stretched out across the old bottles and bags. It started to panic, spraying water desperately from its blowhole. Its mate splashed around nearby making high-pitched trills that sounded like cries for help. A grey-coloured baby dolphin also popped its head up a few metres away.

'Oh no!' cried Bud. 'Quick, we need to help.'

Helen grabbed Skye and immediately lowered him over the port side, in between two bright orange life buoys. She then placed Bud on Skye's head.

'Hold on,' said Helen. 'Are you ready?'

'I can't go in the water, I'll drown. What are you doing?' screamed Bud.

'Like you said, you're going to help that dolphin,' she said. 'Now, go!'

Bud didn't have time to think before Helen dropped Skye into the water. Bud held on tightly as the solid mahogany walking stick plunged vertically into the water before bobbing up again.

'Yuck,' cried Bud as he spat the salty sea-water out from his little mouth.

Skye tried to cross the narrow gap between the barge and the plastic debris but was pushed back by the strong, dangerous undercurrents. One of the eagles screeched overhead.

'Hold on, Bud,' cried Helen, moving her hands in wave-like

formations away from her, like a tai-chi master. 'You can do it.'

Helen's eyes glistened emerald green in the mid-morning light. As if by magic, Skye surged forward against the powerful force of the waves. Wow! A sea horse, thought Bud as they approached the stranded dolphin.

'Jump on to the rubbish, Bud,' shouted Helen. 'Now!'

'I can't! I'm too small,' said Bud.

Skye whinnied impatiently as Bud hesitated. It then lunged deeper into the water and shot up powerfully, throwing Bud into the air.

'Help!' cried Bud as he landed on an old plastic bottle of orange juice with a loud crack.

The dolphin squealed as it saw Bud land just next to it. As it struggled to escape it became more and more weary. The baby dolphin whistled desperately for its dying father.

'Start pushing it back in the water,' said Helen. 'Quickly!'

'How?' he shouted back.

He was so small. How could he help? He knew he had to do something, he had to try. Bud placed his tiny hands on the dolphin's smooth cheeks. The dolphin lay very still now and it looked sadly at Bud, its eyes starting to droop. The white egret spotted Bud and started to hop towards him. Bud glanced up to see the hungry bird then looked back at the dolphin. With a shout and a heave, Bud pushed with all his strength. High up on the barge, Helen looked like she was pulling an imaginary rope.

The dolphin started to shift backwards before falling with a loud plop into the sea.

'We did it!' said Bud, looking up at Helen. 'I didn't think I was strong enough.'

The dolphins reunited under the barge and made a loud click before disappearing beneath the choppy waves. Bud clambered back onto Skye as the white egret took off from the rubbish and flew towards them. It swooped to catch Bud but he swung underneath Skye's head. The egret banged its beak into the hard wooden body of the walking stick and flew away, slightly disoriented, back towards the plastic island. Skye swam hard to catch the barge which was now a lot further away. Avoiding the churning white froth, they arrived at the side of the boat. How were they going to get back up now? Bud was looking at everything upside down. Skye bobbed enthusiastically in the water awaiting his mistress' next order as Bud scampered onto the top of its head. The saltwater spray from the boat's stern covered Bud. The barge was moving quicker than it looked! Out of the corner of his eye, Bud saw a black dorsal fin zig-zagging towards them. A huge pair of outstretched jaws lunged out of the water. It was a tiger shark about three metres long from nose to tail. Its teeth were arranged like rows of sharp, broken glass. The shark went straight for Skye's head. The stubborn colt saw the danger and snorted with defiance, swivelling instantly and turning black with rage, nearly knocking Bud into the sea.

'A shark,' cried Bud, clutching the slippery handle. 'Help!'

The shark's eyes were cold and lifeless as it moved in. Skye outmanoeuvred it by leaping away from the rows of killer teeth bearing down. The shark crashed back into the sea and started to circle its prey for the next attack. It wouldn't be long.

'Hit the shark on the nose, Skye,' said Bud, struggling to reign in the wild seahorse.

As Skye moved frantically through the waves, Bud started to feel dizzy but kept his grip and scanned the water.

'It's coming back,' he shouted as it cut through the surf towards them. 'Jump! Now!'

Just as the tiger shark made another desperate effort, Skye leapt out of the water and bopped it on the nose. Bud was so close he could almost touch the smooth grey skin of the apex predator. Skye snorted as they watched the tiger shark lurk back underneath the cloud of white water. Thank goodness for that. Bud's hands were still shivering. He looked up at smiling emerald eyes twinkling at him.

'Skye! Wrap the rope around your head,' said Helen.

Helen threw down a rope and Skye managed to wrap his head round it enough times for the rag-picker to pull them to safety. The two heroes were soon on the barge again. Bud fell into Helen's warm palm and shook himself dry.

'Thank you,' Bud squealed.

'Well done, Bud. Are you okay?'

'Yes, that was amazing but how did you save the dolphin?'

'With your help and a bit of magic,' said Helen, patting Skye's head.

Chapter Thirteen
The Island

Just before midday, the old barge sailed around the south of Lantau Island, passing Fan Lau Lighthouse before continuing eastwards, travelling slower than before. Bud gazed at the beautiful beaches stretching for miles and longed to be a boy again so he could build sandcastles and paddle in the sea. A short distance away, on the starboard side, a tiny island came into view. There was a port surrounded by tall buildings in a horseshoe shape. It looked very new and sparkled in the warm sun. On all sides of the port, dense jungle canopy covered the island in a sea of green. The barge slowed and heaved and groaned under the weight of its enormous cargo as it made its approach. Standing downwind, Bud was struggling with the awful smell as Helen walked towards the front of the barge. He really wanted to be a boy again but was in a helpless situation. He looked up at Helen who was humming gently. She looked even younger than before. Why wasn't she helping him?

'When are you going to change me back to a boy?'

'What makes you think I can help?' asked Helen.

'You have magic powers,' said Bud.

'Really? Anyway, not yet,' replied Helen.

'Why?' Bud shouted. 'I helped the pink dolphin, didn't I?'

'It's almost time to get off,' said Helen, smiling down at Bud.

Bud crossed his arms and sighed. It was better not to argue with her, Bud decided. She might turn him into a frog and leave him on this island forever! He didn't want to be eaten by a snake.

'How long has this rubbish been on the boat for?' said Bud.

'One to two days,' said Helen. 'The rubbish is sorted, processed and stored in containers before being loaded onto the barge and shipped here.'

Thick black tyres hanging from the barge's hull scraped against the stone walls of the jetty. The barge slowly came to a halt. Helen picked up Skye and placed Bud in the top pocket of her ragged grey blouse. A huge blue crane and a long line of flatbed trucks were queuing to ferry the rubbish to the landfill site.

'You'll see more from up there,' she said. 'Cheer up! Let's go and get your friends.'

'Okay! Brrr, it's windy up here,' Bud said.

High above the port, a dozen diggers busily quarried the stone from the rocky summit. Towards the far end of the port, construction workers dropped the quarried stone into the water next to the port area with loud crashes.

'Why are they doing that?' asked Bud.

'They need to make the island bigger,' said Helen. 'It's called land reclamation.'

'Why?' said Bud.

'If they make the port bigger, then more barges can unload

their cargo at the same time,' said Helen.

'Why don't they just produce less rubbish?' said Bud.

'Good point, Bud, but easier said than done,' said Helen, smiling.

In the distance, Bud saw a tall white building with a beautiful wave-like design.

'Is that the incinerator?' Bud asked.

'Yes.'

'Do they burn all the rubbish here?' asked Bud

'Burning rubbish isn't good for the environment so we need to be careful about what we burn and what we bury in a landfill,' replied Helen. 'Come on, or we'll miss them.'

More questions bubbled to the surface of Bud's busy mind. Why do we create rubbish if we just end up burning or burying it? Bud imagined a sea full of plastic bottles, plastic bags, surgical masks, sweet wrappers, crisp packets and other rubbish. Bud hopped from one plastic island to another, avoiding the dead fish, dolphins and other marine life.

'If we create rubbish, it's important to dispose of it properly,' said Bud. 'For the environment.'

'That's why we're here,' said Helen. 'To educate you about the consequences of being a litter bug.'

Helen watched as a small yellow digger scooped the loose refuse out of the port side of the barge and placed it into an empty container on the first truck. She hopped off the barge and walked to the side of the truck. As the digger's powerful jaws shovelled the debris into the truck, Helen held Skye in position like a grey heron at the side of a fast-flowing river. The horse was motionless and his eyes were fixed on the falling waterfall of waste above. Then, he darted in and fished out an old shoebox.

'Are my friends in there?' said Bud.

Helen smiled, took the broken box and walked towards the office buildings at the far end of the quayside. Bud clambered out of the pocket and shuffled down Helen's arm to get a closer look. She opened the lid carefully and huddled inside were Daring Mr Cockroach, Old Mr Rat, Miss Worm, Fruity, Crazy Cola and Mickey Mosquito. They were still sleeping. A few seconds later, as the sunlight streamed in, they woke up and shielded their eyes from the powerful rays.

'You're safe,' squealed Bud as he jumped up and down, nearly falling.

'Bud, is that you?' asked Miss Worm.

'Yes. It's me!' he cried.

They chatted excitedly and began to help Old Mr Rat to his feet. Helen then peered down into the depths and smiled. Her teeth flashed brightly. The friends jumped back. Helen lifted Skye up to have a look and he snorted, turning deep-amber orange.

'Who's that?' shouted the friends huddling together again around Old Mr Rat.

'It's okay,' shouted Bud. 'They won't hurt you.'

'My name's Helen and this is Skye,' she said. 'Are you all right?'

'A bit bashed and bruised but we're fine, thank you, Helen,' replied Old Mr Rat.

'You've had quite an adventure so I thought it best to let you sleep first,' said Helen. 'You must be tired.'

'Where are you taking us?' asked Daring Mr Cockroach, peering out of the side of the box.

'Back home, on the next barge' said Helen. 'The alley is too dangerous so I'm relocating you all to the park across the road. You'll be safe there.'

'She knows where we live!' said Mickey Mosquito.

'I've always wanted to go to the park,' said Miss Worm. 'I can play in the soil, instead of the rubbish. My friends say it's much healthier.'

'And I can dance in the autumn leaves under the apple trees,' said Fruity.

'Would that be okay for you all?' said Helen.

'Great!' chorused the friends.

'Thank you very much, Helen,' said Old Mr Rat. 'That's very kind of you.'

'You're very welcome,' she said. 'Before we leave though, I thought I'd show you around the island first to see what happens to rubbish.'

'I want to go back now,' said Daring Mr Cockroach, growing slightly impatient.

'Lead on, Helen,' said Old Mr Rat.

'Let's go,' said Crazy Cola.

They entered an empty lift inside the nearest office building and, as it climbed higher, Bud was the first to see the summit of the hill and the never-ending hole sprawled deep at the bottom of the quarry. He stood on his tiptoes to get a better view but felt uneasy and his head started to pound again. As the lift climbed, Bud's heartbeat raced and his hands began to sweat. The lift stopped abruptly at the top floor with a shudder. Bud did well not to fall off Helen's arm as the doors flung open and she walked out into a bright corridor with windows on both sides. She placed the soggy shoebox on a nearby cabinet and the friends peered out.

'This is the landfill site, where the rubbish is buried,' said Helen, pointing towards the quarry.

The whole area was huge and the shape looked like an open-air football stadium, but much bigger. An army of trucks, forklift trucks, bulldozers, diggers and cranes were busy. Some tipped metal containers of endless tonnes of rubbish into the giant monster's mouth, whilst some smoothed over the rubbish, crushing and pressing it down. High above the quarry, two drones whizzed from one side to the other taking photos. Even from where they stood, the noise from the landfill was loud. The friends stared in complete silence for over two minutes, focussing intently on the furious activity below. The air became tense. They were thinking the same as him, Bud decided. That they were lucky to be alive.

'We were nearly goners,' said Daring Mr Cockroach.

'I'm glad that we didn't go in there,' said Bud. 'We'd never escape!'

'I want to go down and have a closer look,' said Crazy Cola.

'WHAT!' cried Daring Mr Cockroach, almost falling off the cabinet.

'Just kidding!' said Crazy Cola. 'Even I'm not that silly.'

'To your left is the rubbish incinerator,' said Helen, pointing to the tall, white building behind the quarry. 'Don't worry, this is as close as we'll get.'

'Thank goodness for that,' said Fruity.

'What happens to the rubbish after it's been incinerated?' asked Bud, still staring at the quarry.

'The rubbish is turned into ash and is then taken by barge to another landfill,' said Helen, looking at her watch. 'We need to go.'

'Are we going to another landfill?' said Miss Worm, looking worried.

'No, we are going on the barge back home. Now let's go back down,' said Helen. 'It's almost time.'

Helen hurried into the lift with the friends safely tucked back into their makeshift home. They arrived back at the jetty and started to chatter like hungry chicks in a nest. Another barge had been loaded with its cargo of ash in strong, metal containers and was preparing to embark on the return trip to Kowloon. The sun was high in the sky now as the sailors did their final checks. Helen looked down at the friends and began walking towards the entrance to the barge.

'The return journey should be quicker as the sea lanes are quieter now,' she said.

'Hurray!' cried the party, bobbing up and down.

Back in Helen's pocket, Bud looked out over the rocky shore surrounding the jetty on both sides. The waves crashed against the rocks and stone wall and splashed several feet in the air. With every new wave, small pieces of rubbish would be left clinging to the rocks like plastic seaweed.

'There's rubbish everywhere! I can't wait to be a boy again. I can help to tidy it up.'

Just then, Bud looked down to his right and saw something unusual.

'Helen, what's that, over there?'

Helen was on the barge now and didn't hear. The sound of the engines had drowned out Bud's tiny voice. A few metres away, on a slippery rock lay a beautiful baby white egret, struggling to escape from the discarded fishing nets that clung cruelly to its neck. It was slowly dying.

'Oh no,' cried Bud. 'I've got to help it.'

Bud leapt up and clambered down Helen's arm once more. If he didn't try, it wouldn't survive.

'Helen, we've got to...'

Just then, a strong gust of wind snatched him away and into the air towards the cold, hungry waves.

'Help!' cried Bud.

Chapter Fourteen
The Baby Egret

Two white wings from behind him opened instinctively and started to move up and down in a quick but controlled fashion. Everything happened very quickly and, before he knew it, Bud felt himself moving upwards.

'I'm flying!' he shouted, as he glided effortlessly over the jetty wall.

The wind dropped and Bud wobbled nervously as he saw the dark-coloured waves gnashing and gnarling just a few metres below. He twisted and tumbled, struggling to control his new wings. He didn't know how to fly. The wings had a mind of their own. All he could do was hold on tight and hope for a soft landing. He looked down. The egret was still struggling on the rocks.

'Woah,' he cried, swinging from side to side.

He remembered being seasick on the barge and now he was flying, which felt a lot worse. Another powerful gust threw Bud high above the port and he could make out the tiny figure of Helen walking up and down the side of the barge, holding the shoe box and looking towards the entrance of the barge. She must know Bud was lost. Was she going to help him? He must get to the bird first, decided Bud.

'Wheee!'

Bud dived towards the ailing bird. He braced himself and crash-landed onto a sharp, wet rock next to the egret and the long, twisted fishing nets it was caught in. Bud's two little wings instinctively closed and went back inside their shell.

'My back!' he said, picking himself up and rubbing his shell.

The bird saw Bud and cried out.

SQUAWK! SQUAWK!

It was just a chick but it still towered above Bud and its beady eyes stared fiercely at him. The egret might gobble up Bud before he had a chance to try and help it. The force of the waves was pulling the fishing nets and the bird back into the cruel sea. With each struggle, the egret was tiring itself out. Bud had to do something quickly.

BOOOOOOOOM! BOOOOOOOOM! BOOOOOOOOM!

The horn of the departing barge was deafening.

'It's leaving, without me,' Bud cried.

His stomach began to churn like the waves around him and his little hands started to shake, worse than before.

'What am I going to do?' he said. 'Shall I fly back? Helen, help!'

There was no answer. Bud crouched down and put his head in his hands, trying to escape all the troubles in his life. Flashbacks of playing in the sand with his parents haunted him. He then looked at the dying egret. It had stopped moving. He needed to help it first, but how? Bud slid over to the bird and placed his hands on the smooth white feathers near its neck. He tried to pull the net away but it was impossible to remove. It was too tight. He needed to bite through it and make a hole or else the poor thing would perish within minutes. The salty spray of a large wave soaked Bud and the bird. He looked up and saw the barge chug steadily out of the port. He was really on his own now. He put his head down and continued. Wave after wave bombarded him as if trying to persuade him to give up.

'Keep going!' he said.

Sweat began to roll off Bud's forehead as he toiled to help the desperate bird. He worked faster with an energy he didn't know he had. The nets began to break and a little hole appeared around its neck. It was working! The egret's little black eyes opened once more and started to roll around slowly. Then it jerked its head from side to side. Just a little bit more, thought Bud as he continued to chew through the net with his tiny but sharp little teeth.

'That's it!'

He stood up, caught his breath and wiped his head. The hole was now big enough for the egret to shake off the net and it struggled gingerly to its feet. Almost immediately, another hungry wave gobbled up the net into the murky depths. The chick flopped forwards and its beady eyes stared fiercely at Bud once again. It looked hungry. Bud backed off as it stretched its long, white wings and suddenly realised that his charity might backfire on him.

'Thank you very much,' said the egret. 'Phew! That was close!'

'Are you going to eat me?' asked Bud.

'Not at all, you saved my life,' the bird said. 'I'm Eric, lovely to meet you.'

Eric gave a little bow and shook one of Bud's tiny hands with his wing.

'It was nothing. I'm Bud, nice to meet you too. Why are you out here all alone?'

'I came out looking for some lunch but then I got tired and lost,' said Eric. 'I was resting on these rocks when I got caught up in a fishing net.'

'Do your parents know you're here?' said Bud.

'My parents are dead,' Eric said as he wiped away a tear.

'Oh, I'm sorry,' said Bud.

'That's okay, you didn't know,' said Eric.

'What happened to them?' said Bud.

'They choked on two white plastic bottle tops floating in the water,' said Eric. 'They thought they were fish. Now, I'm on my own.'

Eric leaned against the rocks, turned away and burst into tears. Bud patted him on the back.

'Where do you live, Eric?' asked Bud. 'We'd better try and get off these rocks. They're treacherous.'

'I've lived in lots of places,' said Eric. 'My parents moved around a lot. Hong Kong Park, Hong Kong Wetland Park, Mai Po Nature Reserve. Eventually, they settled in Tsim Sha Tsui, under the Star

Ferry pier. How about you?'

'I live in Kwai Fong,' said Bud.

'Never been there,' said Eric, standing up again. 'How will you get back?'

'I don't know,' said Bud. 'I suppose I'll need to fly.'

'Fly!' cried Eric. 'It's such a long way and you're so small. Come on, hop on, I'll take you.'

The adventures of the last two days had started to catch up with Bud and he was too exhausted to refuse. The wind had picked up and it was too dangerous to stay on the rocks any longer. Another wave almost swept little Bud away as it hit the rock and smashed into a thousand little pieces, like liquid glass. A large orange fiddler crab scuttled out of the boiling foam and onto the rock opposite them. Its huge left claw effortlessly snapped through the tough seaweed lying around. It stared at him with hungry, sharp eyes and moved towards them. Bud climbed onto Eric's neck and quickly got into position.

'I don't want to stay a second longer, Eric,' said Bud. 'Are you ready?'

'Ready?' shouted Eric. 'Let's go!'

Chapter Fifteen
The Return Trip

Eric shook the spray from his wings, stood back and took three long, gangly strides forwards.

SNAP!

'OWWW! That hurt!' cried Eric, jumping into the air, its long thin legs and wings waving clumsily.

The fiddler crab had pinched Eric on the leg and was hustling underneath them menacingly, doing a sort of nervous dance as it went from side to side. Bud closed his eyes, buried his head in the warm feathers and clung on. Eric landed on one leg, leaping around trying his best to avoid the harsh click-clacking of the crab's powerful pincer. He took off again, more smoothly this time, and left the unfriendly crab standing alone on the slippery rocks. A second later, a large wave swept it back into the sea.

'It's okay, Bud. We're on our way,' said Eric.

Bud opened his eyes again and the view below was magnificent. The water seemed serene and flat and far off in the distance, he could even see the beautiful view of Victoria Harbour and its whirl of skyscrapers. However, the cold sea breeze quickly shook him from his aerial reverie.

'How am I going to find Helen now?' he cried. 'I'll never be a boy again.'

As the adrenaline rush began to fade, Bud's cold and tired bones ached even more. An aeroplane whizzed overhead making holes in the marshmallow-like clouds. Bud's huge lollipop sun was nowhere to be seen either. Hundreds of metres below, seagulls flew together in the distance noisily following the wake of a fast-moving boat.

'It's the barge,' cried Bud.

He pointed at the small dot below. 'Eric, can you take me to it?'

'Hang on,' he shouted, nose-diving towards the barge and the open sea.

The animated figure of Helen was clearly visible now, as Eric zoomed overhead and landed gently on the railings of the barge next to her. Bitter tears started to roll down Bud's soft cheeks. He'd missed his mysterious new friend and his alley pals.

'Helen!' cried Bud.

'Well done, Bud,' said Helen, stroking Eric's smooth head. 'I knew you could do it.'

'You knew! So you left me there on purpose?'

'Thank you, Eric,' said Helen. 'Please be more careful next time with fishing nets though.'

'Will do. Goodbye everyone!' shouted Eric, as he took off again.

'Safe journey home,' said Helen, waving.

Helen held Bud in her soft, warm hand and placed a tiny little scarf around his neck. Bud's head was still spinning and Helen was chuckling mischievously. She seemed to be enjoying it all.

'What's going on?' said Bud. 'Is this all a game to you?'

Everyone smiled at Bud and Helen gave him a warm drink and a tiny little piece of chocolate. Bud played with his fingers again nervously.

'You left me there to die, didn't you?' he said.

'No,' said Helen.

'I'm never going to be a boy again, am I?

Helen winked at Skye and the walking stick giddied and rattled on the rail. Lightning tore the sky in two and thunder rumbled around them like the drums of an angry sea god. Out of nowhere, a storm surged forwards. Helen clicked her fingers and quietly recited some strange words in a foreign tongue. Bud looked out at a giant maelstrom whirling towards them like the apocalypse.

'Ahh!' cried the friends as they huddled together in the shoebox.

Like a conductor's baton, Helen directed Skye in the air and conjured another flash of lightning. She seemed to be urging the storm towards her. Another huge clap of thunder made Bud jump. Helen opened her hand. The snake-like outline of Stonecutters Bridge was now visible as the barge neared its destination. Bud trembled and his head was starting to spin again.

'Help,' cried Bud as the maelstrom scooped him up and into the waterspout.

It spun Bud around three times but Bud didn't feel any pain or discomfort. It was like being in a giant carwash ride at a funfair.

'This is fun,' he shouted, flying around just above the barge. 'Wheee.'

His friends looked on nervously as Helen waved her hands in the air and opened her sparkling eyes. A few minutes later, the storm dissipated and Bud was sitting on the seat next to her. He was a boy again!

'I'm a boy!' he shouted. 'I'm a boy!'

Bud jumped around checking his four limbs were real and back to normal. His shell and antennae had gone and he was almost the same height as Helen, the same as before.

'Hooray,' cried the friends as they gazed at the giant next to them.

'He's not crazy after all,' said Crazy Cola.

'He really is a boy,' said Daring Mr Cockroach.

Crazy Cola and Daring Mr Cockroach scratched their heads in disbelief. Bud was still leaping around like a fawn learning how to walk when Helen strode over to him.

'Remember next time, Bud,' she said. 'Don't drop litter.'

'I'm a boy again! I'm a boy again!'

'Bud!' said Helen.

Bud calmed down and sat next to her. He patted Skye's head and looked around. The barge had slowed and a long, loud blast of its horn signalled its arrival at the Transfer Station. On the quayside, a flurry of trucks and diggers loaded a new mountain of rubbish into a long blue container. Seagulls screamed overhead and the sun shone brightly.

'Thank you, Helen!' Bud smiled sincerely. 'You really used magic, didn't you?'

She shone an emerald smile and gazed down at the friends in the shoebox looking up nervously at the seagulls.

'I hope they won't see us,' cried Fruity, holding onto Old Mr Rat.

'They won't get you, you're safe with me,' said Helen.

Bud smiled down at his friends. Miss Worm smiled and a tear rolled down her soft cheek.

'Let's take your friends back home, shall we?' said Helen. 'Then it's time for you to go home, too, Bud.'

'YEAH!' cried Bud, still lost in the moment.

'Is that yours?' said Helen, pointing to a little blue rucksack that had suddenly appeared on the metal seat.

'My bag!' said Bud, rushing back to pick it up.

'I also found your phone under a car outside my sweet shop, Bud,' said Helen. 'Please be more careful next time.'

Bud took his phone and immediately thought of his parents. The clock on the phone read four o'clock in the afternoon on the ninth of October. That was strange. It was as if time had stopped after he had entered Strangely Sweet. He put on his cashmere scarf and replied to Mum's message.

'I'm on my way home, Mum. See you soon. Bud.'

One minute later, Mum replied, 'Ok!'. The group disembarked and crossed the road to the bus stop to take them back to Kwai Fong. As the bus sped towards its destination, Bud fell asleep, completely exhausted from his exploits and too tired to think. He was finally on his way home.

Chapter Sixteen

A Lesson Learned

The bus arrived in Kwai Fong, Helen and Bud alighted, crossed the road and headed towards the entrance of the park. On the way, they passed two big shopping malls and the dark and dirty alley. A warm autumn wind blew as they continued through the park, past the basketball courts.

'Almost there,' said Helen.

Despite being a boy again, after what felt like an eternity, Bud started to have that sinking feeling again in his stomach as the group reached a large banyan tree in the centre of the park. Its long roots sprawled out many metres away from its centuries-old trunk. Birds sang brightly from its highest branches and Bud saw the bushy tail of a brown squirrel disappear into a hole. Helen gently placed the shoebox on a nearby root and the group peered out for the first time at their new home. Bees and butterflies busied themselves in the flower beds near the main group of trees.

'Oooh! It's just like I imagined it would be,' said Fruity.

'Will I ever see you again?' said Bud.

Miss Worm turned away and sobbed quietly whilst everyone else looked at Old Mr Rat. He smiled softly at Bud with wise eyes and then looked around him slowly. He had seen a lot of the world and didn't want to disappoint young Bud.

'Never say never, Bud,' he said. 'But we must say farewell, for now.'

'Goodbye, Bud,' said the group. 'We'll never forget you.'

'Goodbye my friends,' said Bud. 'Me too.'

'Goodbye everyone,' said Helen. 'Please take care and enjoy your new home.'

'Thank you for everything, Helen,' said Old Mr Rat. 'Until we meet again.'

'Now hurry everyone! We have much to do,' said Old Mr Rat as the group quickly disappeared into the safety of the ancient tree.

Helen picked up the shoebox, checked it was empty and threw it into the nearest rubbish bin. When she returned, Bud was sitting on a nearby bench and crying. He looked up at Helen.

'I'll never see them again, will I?' he said.

'Like Old Mr Rat said, never say never, Bud. Let's go,' said Helen, patting him softly on the shoulder. 'It's been a long day.'

'But there's so much litter,' said Bud. 'Let me tidy it up, first.'

Bud dried his eyes and spent several minutes tidying up the rubbish near the base of the great banyan tree. As he trudged back to Strangely Sweet with Helen, he turned back to see Miss Worm waving at him inside one of the tree's giant knots. Bud's spirits lifted and he waved back, smiling. Bud was eager to get home but had many questions for Helen. When they arrived back at the sweet shop, the gangly spider scuttled around on its silken web, looking for flies. High up in the rafters, the brown owl moved its head and screeched, its large eyes surveying the entire shop.

'It's nice to be back,' said Helen.

The ancient woman then closed the door, turned on the lights and walked across the dusty floor. The rows of sweets in their glass jars sparkled and she placed Skye carefully on the counter. She washed her hands, made a cup of tea for herself and Bud and sat down to read. Something above the door had caught Bud's eye and he stared at it silently for a few seconds.

'That wasn't there last time, was it?' he said, enjoying the warmth of the cup in his cold hands.

A mysterious black and white clock with a yin-yang symbol in the middle was hanging near the doorbell. On it were three small clocks on the bottom, all telling a different time. The main clock read four o'clock in the afternoon on the ninth of October. It was very confusing. Helen glanced up and a strong gust of cool wind whistled under the door. Bud trembled with the familiar feeling that Helen knew what he was thinking. Very strange. He opened his bag and looked at his phone again. The time once again read four o'clock in the afternoon on the ninth of October.

DING! DING! DING! DING!

The ancient grandfather clock chimed four times, its solemn tones echoing through the shop. The owl flew out of sight, disturbed by the vibrations.

'Four o'clock,' said Bud. 'But it feels like I've been away forever.'

'I stopped time once you came into my shop,' said Helen, casually putting down her book and sipping her hot tea. 'Now it's started again, see!'

'You what?' said Bud, almost dropping his phone.

Helen picked up Skye and tapped him gently on the floor.

'I stopped time and may need to do the same next time as well,' she said turning away.

'I love my little Skye, don't I!' said Helen, stroking the horse's smooth head. 'You've been a good boy, haven't you?'

Skye whinnied and turned a deep mahogany.

'Next time?' asked Bud.

'Well, you are coming back, aren't you?' said Helen. 'Each adventure is different.'

Helen chuckled with her familiar laugh, piercing him once more with her emerald eyes. Bud stroked Skye's smooth head. One answer led to another question. How did Helen stop time? Is that possible? Did he really want to come back to this strange place with this mysterious old woman? His eyes lit up as a new world and its infinite possibilities opened up before his eyes.

'Yes, yes of course,' said Bud. 'But I don't want to be a litter bug again.'

'Well that depends on you, doesn't it?' said Helen. 'See you next Saturday afternoon at four o'clock then and don't be late.'

'See you then.' said Bud.

'Oh, and please invite James and Jenny to join too,' said Helen.

Bud ran down the street, and before long, was outside the school gates. He stopped only to pick up the litter he saw flying around. What an adventure! Did time really stand still? Was it all real or just a crazy dream? His mind raced as he ran through the square and turned the corner into his estate where a beautiful rainbow beamed overhead welcoming him in a blaze of colour. Just then, as if by magic once more, Bud heard Helen's voice in the whistling wind. This time the message was very clear.

'Remember next time, Bud. Don't drop litter.'

'Okay,' said Bud as he arrived underneath his flat.

Bud rang the doorbell and Mum answered. Bud felt like he hadn't seen her for years but Mum's reaction was the same as always.

'Bud, there you are!' said Mum. 'Come in. Are you hungry?'

'Hi Mum,' said Bud. 'Yes, I'm famished. I'll just have a shower and get changed first.'

Fifteen minutes later, Bud was sat on the sofa eating a steaming hot bowl of spicy noodles. Dad sauntered in, sat down and turned on the television. He whistled his favourite tune as he waited, turned to Bud and smiled.

'Let's watch the weather report, shall we?' said Dad.

'Good idea, Dad,' said Bud.

'At eight o' clock this evening, the typhoon signal number eight will be hoisted. The name of this Typhoon is Helen. Take care everyone and be sure to stay indoors,' said the news reporter.

Dad turned off the television and started to read the newspaper. Bud chuckled. The sun shone through the windows as he finished off his food and stared at the fruit bowl. Inside was one apple and three oranges.

'Hi, Fruity,' he said. 'Don't worry, I won't eat you!'

He started to peel an orange. The clock on the mantelpiece read four forty-five. It was all true then. It wasn't a dream. He finished off the orange and gazed out of the window. If he told his parents, they'd never believe him. He called James.

'Hello, Bud,' said James.

'Hi James, I'm thinking of arranging a *No Litter Lunchtime* campaign at school next week,' he said. 'What do you think?'

Several seconds passed in silence.

'Unbelievable!' said James. 'I can't believe you would actually think of this. I'm in. Can Jenny join us, too?'

'Of course, that's what I was going to suggest,' said Bud. 'We can also organise *Litter Free Days* on Saturday and Sunday mornings near our school if you like?'

'Wow,' cried James. 'Where did you suddenly get all these ideas from?'

'I'll tell you later,' said Bud. 'It's a secret!'

THE END

Acknowledgements

Thank you to my wife and all my family for their constant love and support without which this book would not have come to fruition.

Sincere thanks to Sandra Glover and everyone at Cornerstones.

My deepest thanks and respect to Dr. Cheri Chan for her wonderful support and encouragement from my PDGE days to writing the foreword of this book.

Thank you to all students and colleagues both past and present at Buddhist Lim Kim Tian Memorial Primary School. It was you who first supported 'The Litter Bug' as an English Drama Club production in 2016!

A very big thank you to my good friend Miss Kay Wong for her wonderful illustrations that really bring the story to life.

About the Author

Sam Barbour has worked as a primary school teacher in Hong Kong since 2007. He is also an award-winning singer-songwriter and his music has been played on the BBC and in over 25 countries across 6 continents. Originally from the UK, he loves creating original English teaching resources for children such as chants, songs, poems and drama scripts. *The Litter Bug* is his first book for children. His YouTube channel **Teacher Ham** has accrued over 2 million views.

www.sambarbour.com
www.youtube.com//TeacherHam